TUSK TUSK

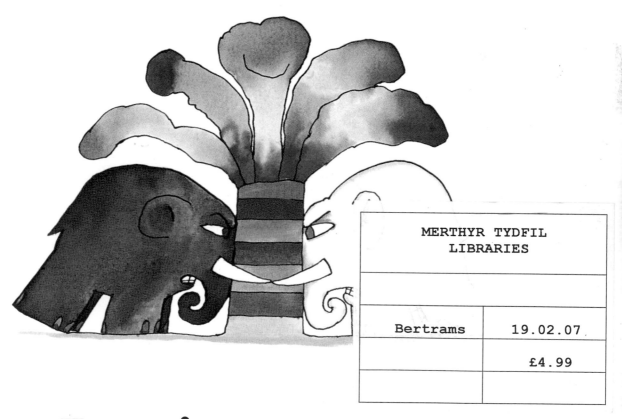

David McKee

Andersen Press • London

Once, all the elephants in the world were black

MERTHYR TYDFIL PUBLIC LIBRARIES

PERIOD OF LOAN : This book must be returned within twenty one days of issue unless renewed.

RENEWALS : A loan may be renewed by (i) delivering book to be re-dated; or (ii) informing the Library of its Issue No. and the latest date on the Issue Label. Books required by other readers cannot be renewed.

FINES : As displayed in Library.

GIVE NOTICE OF ANY CHANGE OF ADDRESS AT ONCE

G. H. JAMES B A., A L A
LIBRARIES OFFICER

Bedlinog P.	31/12/07	

THIS BOOK MUST BE RETURNED OR RENEWED BEFORE THE LAST DATE MENTIONED ABOVE.

Vive la différence!

Copyright © David McKee, 1978. This paperback edition first published in 2006 by Andersen Press Ltd.

The rights of David McKee to be identified as the author and illustrator of this work have been asserted by him in accordance with the

Copyright, Designs and Patents Act, 1988. First published in Great Britain in 1978 by Andersen Press Ltd., 20 Vauxhall Bridge Road, London SW1V 2SA.

Published in Australia by Random House Australia Pty., 20 Alfred Street, Milsons Point, Sydney, NSW 2061.

All rights reserved. Colour separated in Switzerland by Photolitho AG, Zürich. Printed and bound in Italy by Grafiche AZ, Verona.

10 9 8 7 6 5 4 3 2 1

British Library Cataloguing in Publication Data available.

ISBN-10: 1 84270 579 2   ISBN-13: 978 1 84270 579 7

This book has been printed on acid-free paper

or white. They loved all creatures,

but they hated each other,

and each kept to his own side of the jungle.

One day the black elephants decided
to kill all the white elephants,

and the white ones decided to kill the black.

The peace-loving elephants from each side
went to live deep in the darkest jungle.

They were never seen again.

A battle began.

It went on...

and on, and on…

until all the elephants were dead.

For years no elephants were seen in the world.

Then, one day, the grandchildren of the peace-loving

elephants came out of the jungle. They were grey.

Since then the elephants have lived in peace.

have been giving each other strange looks.

Other books by
David McKee

The Conquerors

Elmer

Four Red Apples

Mr Benn – Gladiator

Not Now, Bernard

Three Monsters

Two Can Toucan

Who is Mrs Green?

Isabel's Noisy Tummy